Extraordinary Praise for Lori Rader-Day

"Lori Rader-Day is a modern-day Agatha Christie: her mysteries are taut, her characters are real and larger than life, and her plots are relentlessly surprising."
—Kate Moretti, *New York Times* bestselling author of *The Vanishing Year*

"A brilliant concept, brilliantly told. . . . Living, breathing characters and filled with fresh prose and sharp dialogue."
—Jeffery Deaver, *New York Times* bestselling author

"Fans of Agatha Christie's *And Then There Were None* will be riveted by Rader-Day's latest."
—*Library Journal* (starred review)

"Another signature Lori Rader-Day blend of psychology, suspense, and noir."
—CrimeReads

"Another harrowing nightmare by a master of the sleepless night."
—*Kirkus Reviews*

"Irresistible. . . . A brilliantly absorbing novel from one of my favorite new crime writers."
—Sheena Kamal, internationally bestselling author of *The Lost Ones*

"I was riveted . . . twists that keep coming up until the final breathtaking reveal."
—Hallie Ephron, *New York Times* bestselling author of *Careful What You Wish For*

DEATH AT GREENWAY

Also by Lori Rader-Day

The Lucky One
Under a Dark Sky
The Day I Died
Little Pretty Things
The Black Hour

DEATH AT GREENWAY

A Novel

LORI RADER-DAY

wm

WILLIAM MORROW

An Imprint of HarperCollinsPublishers

P.S.™ is a trademark of HarperCollins Publishers.

DEATH AT GREENWAY. Copyright © 2021 by Lori Rader-Day. All rights reserved. Printed in the United States of America. No part of this book may be used or reproduced in any manner whatsoever without written permission except in the case of brief quotations embodied in critical articles and reviews. For information, address HarperCollins Publishers, 195 Broadway, New York, NY 10007.

HarperCollins books may be purchased for educational, business, or sales promotional use. For information, please email the Special Markets Department at SPsales@harpercollins.com.

FIRST EDITION

Designed by Diahann Sturge

Library of Congress Cataloging-in-Publication Data has been applied for.

ISBN 978-0-06-293804-6
ISBN 978-0-06-293803-9 (hardcover library edition)
ISBN 978-0-06-309440-6 (international edition)

21 22 23 24 25   LSC   10 9 8 7 6 5 4 3 2 1

For the ten 'vacs of Greenway:
Doreen, Maureen, Beryl, Pamela, Tina, Edward,
and the others whose names we might yet learn,
and to all those who have cared for and kept Greenway

With special thanks to the National Trust
and the staff and volunteers of Greenway House

DEATH AT GREENWAY

PROLOGUE
AGATHA M. C. CHRISTIE MALLOWAN

South Devon, England, 11:15 a.m., 3 September 1939

The mistress of the house was at work on the mayonnaise when the kitchen wireless began to speak of war.

"This morning the British Ambassador in Berlin handed the German Government a final note," the voice said, "stating that, unless we heard from them by eleven o'clock that they were prepared at once to withdraw their troops from Poland, a state of war would exist between us."

The others in the room had fallen silent. Agatha put down the bowl and whisk, the salad forgotten. She smoothed a strand of hair away from her face. Making mayonnaise was a physical task—it got the blood moving as well as calisthenics if done properly, though few put forth the proper effort. She insisted on doing it herself. Down the hall, the infernal 'phone began to ring.

"I have to tell you now that no such undertaking has been received," Chamberlain was saying. *Is it Chamberlain?* Agatha thought his voice sounded quite reedy of late, an old man. "And that consequently," the voice continued, "this country is at war with Germany."

There were no gasps of surprise. At the table her husband

and their friend Mrs. North sat listening, Max leaning forward with elbows on the kitchen table, his pipe jutting out of his mouth. Mrs. Bastin, in from the ferryman's cottage to help with the meal, curled her shoulders over the sink and cried into the vegetables.

"Oh, do be quiet," Max murmured, not as kindly as he might.

Later, Max would probably scoff at Mrs. Bastin's tears. Hadn't they watched the march of war arriving? It was nearly a relief to have the matter decided. What did Mrs. Bastin have to lose? But they all had so much to lose. How could it be war again, so soon?

The 'phone rang, rang. Agatha crossed to the wireless and nudged the dial in time to hear Chamberlain say, "You can imagine what a bitter blow it is to me that all my long struggle to win peace has failed."

She stood back. It put one on notice to have the Prime Minister both hoarse and weary, defeated before they'd begun. She imagined Chamberlain sitting up all night committing these words to the page, to have them ready for the deadline, Parliament's ultimatum for Germany to release Poland from its grip. Would he have made another draft, too, in case the deadline had been met and all was well? They must have known no such plan would be necessary.

"Yet," Chamberlain continued, "I cannot believe that there is anything more or anything different that I could have done and that would have been more successful."

Strange to hear a man so publicly heartbroken. She listened as the PM mustered some vim for the pitch to the country to do their part. What could their part possibly be? She could wrap bandages, she supposed, but the brunt of it would hit the younger set. Rosalind and her friends.

But then even Max was all of thirty-five. Of all the reasons not to marry a younger man—she had gone through all the reasons—sending another husband off to war hadn't been one of them. When Agatha looked over, he plucked his pipe out of his mouth, his expression exultant. He would want to be a part of it—would be an absolute *nuisance* until he'd been given a job. And where did that leave her?

Agatha lost track of Chamberlain, thinking of distance, of separation. She tugged at her apron and hurried from the kitchen.

"Ange?" Max called after her.

The corridor, then through the house to the front hall, where the arch of light in the scallop window above the front door was bright. It was a fine day; all the worst days were.

She neglected the ringing telephone and opened the door, hesitating in the threshold. Outside, James, the latest of the Sealyham terriers, lay near a garden deckchair, white belly to the sun.

The first dog her father had brought home and placed at her feet, she'd gone nearly catatonic with happiness. She had never been able to take in news—not good news, certainly not bad—without seeking seclusion and letting the new information break upon the old, like the river's edge lapping at the shore.

Behind her, she could still hear Chamberlain. Never mind that now. She will hear his words repeated, reproduced, and read them in the evening edition.

Now she had time to wait out the cloud that passed over the hill and darkened the magnolias. *Magnolia grandiflora.* She had time to let her thoughts catch up, her concerns be absorbed. When she felt she could take it all in, plans began to form. She could call on the dispensary, couldn't she? With a little brushing up, she could be useful, too. And of course there were always books to write. A Christie for Christmas, whether the Christie in question felt like writing or not.

When the cloud passed and the sun shone on the hill again,

Agatha came out from under the portico, leaving the door wide, and crossed the gravel drive. She stood on the hill, chin pointed south toward the sea. She took it in: the river that led, so close, to the Channel; the fact of war; the eventualities. When she turned back, Greenway rose above her, the flat Georgian face catching the light like a temple of old. It seemed delicate to her just now. But hadn't it survived a century and a half? Hadn't it sent its sons to fight untold battles? The cannon mounted down the hill and pointed out toward the River Dart told the story. These grounds had already fended off wars long forgotten.

This time, however, they must expect bombs from the air, gas attacks. A modern war with modern consequences, the likes of which no one had ever seen.

Agatha gazed over the warm white stone, stalwart on the high ledge of the river. An ideal house, a dream house. They'd barely had a chance to settle in, hadn't the chance to be happy here. Now she wondered if they would. A war was a rending, a death of how things had been. She had no concern for her life—but the life she had built? The people she had come to count on? Her marriage? This house.

She had traded her mother's house, the home of her idyllic childhood, to stand on this hill and call this house hers. Winterbrook, their residence in Oxfordshire, was Max's, but Greenway House was hers—hers in a way she knew might be seen as prideful, hers in her heart. Hers at last, since she'd come here as a child with her mother, visiting, walking the grounds that would someday be her own. Clever foreshadowing, *she* thought, credit to the author.

But that meant this was the *beginning* of the story, didn't it? If they were to have a proper story, Greenway stood, Max prevailed, Rosalind thrived, and she, Agatha, strung it all together, a book each year. If they were to have a proper story, then this simply couldn't be the end.

-1-

BRIDGET KELLY

*St. Prisca's Hospital, near St. George's
Gardens, London, early April 1941*

Bridget sat on the bench in the corridor until the matron's door swung wide and the woman's stern face took in the sight of her, her apron marked with blood and bile. The auxiliary nurse who had been sent along as escort, as keeper, stood a good distance away and pretended not to watch for details she would deal out later to the others. Bridget walked alone behind Matron's swishing skirts as though to the gallows.

The matron's parlor was as sterile as any surgery. A chair for visitors stood in front of the desk, but Bridget wasn't invited to take it.

"You know of course you cannot be allowed to continue on," the matron said, settling behind the desk. "Hencewith, a decision must be made."

"Where," Bridget said. Her mouth was dry. "Where shall I be sent, Matron?"

Matron Bailey studied her until Bridget could only imagine she would say the gaol.

"I can scarcely believe it of you," the matron said. "I've seen moments of great potential in you, and now— Do you have anything to say for yourself?"

Bridget nearly collapsed with relief for the opportunity to set it straight. "It must be an error, Matron—"

"Your error."

"No," Bridget said. "No, you see it's a mistake—"

"A mistake is the same as an error, Bridget."

"I mean it's a mistake to believe that I—" She sounded guilty, even to herself. "I administered as I was taught, gave the dose as written. If it was the wrong formulation, then—" She faltered, for she was not sure it would do any good to question the chemist's judgment. "I'm a good nurse."

"You are *not* a nurse," the matron said. "And you're a danger to say you are. A nurse. You're not through your probationary hours yet."

Bridget swallowed hard. "No, Matron."

"Therefore, it was not your job to administer treatment to that soldier."

"Sister Clare was run off her feet and my only thought was to help—"

"You've got to the crux of the problem, well done. Your *only* thought." Matron Bailey's look was heavy. "You're single-minded on the ward, ticking the boxes. I've seen you. Arrogant with your peers, unfeeling with the patients."

Arrogant because she hadn't the time to chatter with the others? Because she didn't want to gossip or bring them back to hers for tea? On the ward . . . she'd only meant to be good at the work, hadn't she?

And unfeeling? Well, she wouldn't deny that. "Yes, Matron."

But even this answer came too quickly, she realized. Too quickly, without consideration. The matron shifted in her chair.

"And your striving with the sisters, reaching too far, going too fast, thinking too highly of one's own opinion . . ." The matron folded her hands together. "Have you considered, perhaps, that nursing may not be your calling? There are some fine positions opening for young women such as yourself in the factories—"

"I want to be a nurse, Matron! Truly I do," she said. "My mam . . ." She had a memory of her mam's hand, knuckles pink from the washing. A fluttering sensation started somewhere within her. "She wanted it for me, Matron. She sacrificed a good deal to make it so. I . . . I want to save lives."

Matron Bailey sat quietly for a moment. "Only as a fully trained nurse would you perhaps have all the tools God has seen fit to give us," she said. "Fully trained and years of service. *Service*, Bridget. We are not the Redeemer, handing down decisions on life and death, playing God—even if . . . even if our mothers desperately wished it for us. What I see is a young woman trying to care for our patients with her fists clenched and her heart closed, and that is no nurse I've ever known. Nurses give care when there's nothing else, giving care, taking care. Care, Bridget, which, heretofore from you, I have seen precisely none."

They made jokes about the matron's pronouncements and timeworn words, calling her the Old Bailey behind her back. Judge of their crimes, warden of their time. But Bridget had only ever wanted to please her, to be useful, needed. Was that striving?

She lowered her head, showing her neck for the blade to drop. "What shall I do, Matron? I would do anything to make it right."

"Make it right?" the matron said. "Second chances are hard to come by in our line. A good man, and a good soldier from all reports."

"He's—dead?"

The matron was silent a moment but Bridget wouldn't look.

Finally she said, "His family will arrive shortly, and I don't know what to tell them."

The flutter inside her began again, somewhere near her heart. She felt as though she were being shaken, gently.

Bridget clasped her hands together under her pinafore in case they trembled. A biological response, she knew from her training. She'd seen soldiers brought in, their hearts running on pure adrenaline when they should have given out. It turns out the same high anxiety that brought soldiers through catastrophe also rushed through the veins of the surgeons and sisters during a stitch-up. A shockingly bad time for one's hands to shake, with only a needle and boiled silk thread keeping a man's guts inside him.

"Are you all right, Bridget?"

"Yes, Matron."

"Have you been . . . run down?"

Bridget kept her face turned to the floor, the better to concentrate. "Matron?"

"Overwhelmed by the attacks each night, after your long shifts here."

"Yes, Matron, I suppose."

"Not sleeping well, headaches? Have you experienced night terrors?"

Bridget finally looked up. She recognized symptoms, diagnosis. She was the best probationer they had, days put in or not. Great potential. "I don't suffer from battle fatigue, Matron. I'm weathering things, same as everyone." Same as everyone, which was badly. But she wasn't crawling the walls, was she? Hadn't resorted to the blue pills they gave to soldiers out of their minds. She had a thought. They'd never say she was, and send her as a lunatic to an asylum? "Missus?"

Matron Bailey, though, was somewhere else. "I just remembered that your mother . . ."

"Yes, Matron," Bridget said and was glad her hands were hidden.

"Yes, erm. You've got on with things, as well as can be expected but—you've encountered the symptoms of shell shock, surely?"

Bridget imagined herself made of stone. "In the patients, Matron."

The other woman seemed to be chewing on some thought. "It's a terrible quandary you've put me in."

"Yes, Matron."

"We can't have the scandal. No one wants to see our brave men survive a war zone only to succumb to an overeager probationer acting on her own orders." The matron's attentions had wandered to the dirty window high in the room that showed the cold white sky outside. "It may not be right to send you," she murmured.

Bridget caught the scent of freedom, as though the window had been cracked open. "Send me?"

"The request is rather urgent . . . Have you had experience with children, Bridget?"

"Matron?"

"Perhaps you helped around at home with siblings?"

Bridget could track the tremor within as it moved outward into her limbs, weakening her knees, numbing her to her fingertips. She concentrated harder. Every drop of blood, every sinew under her skin vibrated, ready to burst. The smallest movement made, the slightest weakness shown.

"Yes, Matron. Five. There were five."

"I . . . I hadn't remembered it was five."

"Four girls and a boy, Matron."

The matron made a small noise in her throat that Bridget had come to know quite well as a condolence. Or something more like an invocation against the same sort of luck.

The matron smoothed a letter flat on her desk. "And you *like* children, then? I mean to say, Bridget, that you could be trusted with children?"

"Whose children, exactly?"

The matron checked the note. "A Mrs. Arbuthnot is seeking my recommendation of someone to accompany some under-fives evacuated to the countryside. She wants a hospital nurse, but a trainee would be able to see to the care of *healthy* children, and I dare say the air will do you some good."

The matron opened her desk and pulled out a piece of paper and a pen.

Bridget didn't want to go to the countryside or take the air. Or spend time near children, in fact. But she had heard the word *recommendation* and felt herself stretch toward it, the barest hope blooming that she might yet get what she wanted.

"Do I have any choice in the matter? Matron?"

"You do, of course," the matron said easily. "You're under no obligation to accept any favor from me. You may seek your own fortune any time you wish."

Cut loose.

"*Or*," the matron said, "you may have this—let's call it a *conditional* reference. Wheretofore you conclude this assignment to Mrs. Arbuthnot's full satisfaction, we shall see about reinstating you—"

Bridget opened her mouth to speak.

"—to begin again, that is." The matron looked back down at the note in progress before her and scrawled a few lines, murmuring to herself. Bridget had another fleeting memory, taking dictation from her mam for the letter sent to her da, telling him of the littlest's arrival and asking him to send his pay packet home for once. Learning too much, too soon, the complications of affection.

"Now." Matron Bailey folded the letter, crisp edges, put it in an envelope, and sealed it. "We are saving you from scandal, Bridget, and rescuing what I hope will be a fruitful career in the field."

Had she put that in the letter? "Yes, Matron. Thank you, Matron."

"On this assignment," the matron said, "you will need to be vigilant—absolutely vigilant, Bridget, for the children's safety, for the sake of your further improvement. Or you shall have to make your own way with no reference at all. Am I clear?"

The matron copied out a telephone exchange from the note on her desk and held out the letter and the number.

Herein lay her future.

Bridget reached for the offering, and the matron looked her up and down. "Put that filthy apron in the rubbish before anyone else sees you," she said. "I shall trust you to see yourself out without delay. Without engaging in idle chatter, Bridget. This arrangement is between the two of us and that letter to Mrs. Arbuthnot."

Bridget pulled the stained garment over her head, rolled it into a ball as she moved across the room, and shoved it to the bottom of the bin at the door. She didn't partake in idle chatter, and none of the others would be looking out for her to do anything but stare and whisper.

Bridget looked down at the envelope in her hand. There was a dark smudge of blood across the flap. Did it matter that the arrangement was private? The scandal was beyond them already.

Dismissed. Disgraced. If she wasn't to be a nurse, she would very well like to know what she would turn out to be.

-2-

BRIDGET KELLY

A few minutes later

Bridget hurried past the looks and whispers—she was a feast for them!—and went to gather her things. Perhaps they would have liked her cloak and kerchief for another girl, but she needed the cloak, the only warm thing she had to wear. She removed the pins from her kerchief at the sink. She had imagined the day she would graduate to the cap, proper nurse, and now it would not happen.

With her cloak buttoned to the neck, she went to toss the kerchief for the laundry. On top of the basket lay a white cap, still crisp. She took it up. Couldn't she try it on?

But the door opened and in came some of the other probationers, pretending they hadn't come to idle and stare. Bridget hid the cap in her pocket and hurried out and toward home.

Home.

At the door to the courtyard, she stopped and held her brow until she got hold of herself again.

When the tear in Bridget's resolve was stitched up and she felt she might once again show her face, she stepped out into the chill and walked away from St. Prisca's, trying not to think it was for the last time.

At the street, Bridget chose to walk instead of waiting for the bus, where she might meet someone she knew or someone who knew her. She had walked the distance many times, early morning, late at night in the pitch dark of the blackout. Even with bombs making well-known landscape foreign overnight, when she ran out of pavement, out of familiar sights, she never made a wrong turn. Her London, remade each night by new destruction.

Her thoughts circled. What would she do?

As she approached the site of the old home place, her scraping footsteps in the rubble slowed, stopped.

Perhaps a change of air *would* do her some good.

She could still see the shape of their building, though it was gone, a thing that may never have existed. The rest of the row still stood and the lane had gone back to life as normal. In the next street, someone's sheets hung heavy and frozen on the line. Here, though, was a blackened crater, a pile of bricks that had once held everything she cared for in the world.

A breeze kicked up, blowing dust across the site. Down at the bottom, a scrap of fabric flapped. The landlady's tablecloth, perhaps. Mrs. Brown had been properly proud of her heirloom cloths.

Mrs. Brown had been out that day.

Someone had picked through the site since she'd last been to visit. There were shapes in the mud where boards and bricks had been wrenched up. Perhaps a few things had been saved, then. She had not been able to see to it herself, of course, thinking that if she'd crawled inside the scene, she might never climb back out. She'd left the lot to the swindlers and thieves, to the chancers. To the neighbors to take their share. She couldn't decide now if she minded a few of their knives were in service at someone else's table or gone to make aeroplanes.

So much was lost, it might as well be everything.

Bridget could feel the curtains twitching along the lane behind her, those deciding whether to invite her in, those who had already decided. She was freezing to her bones, anyway, and the sky threatened to drop another downpour. She couldn't risk sitting in a kitchen in this lane and having tea served to her, stirred by one of her mam's best spoons.

At her rooming house, Bridget let herself in and scurried up the back stairs before Mrs. Mitchell could hail her for the weather or the next week's rent. In her room, she hung the cloak as she always did, set aside the cap she'd taken.

What should she do? She might light the fire, warm up the room. Put on the kettle? She sat on the edge of her bed.

"You had a visitor," came a shaking voice through the wall. The man in the front room was frail, shuffling as far as the shared toilet down the hall and downstairs, only occasionally, for meals.

Not someone from the hospital. Not the police?

"Who was it?" she said.

"Your young man."

"He's not my young man." More gently, she said, "Thank you, Mr. Watson."

"I heard Herself getting the door," he said. "And I heard the visitor say 'Tom,' clear as a bell."

Bridget put her hands on the bed as though to stand.

She hadn't done what they said she had, surely. She had no way of making sense of it. And now her only hope was to care for children in the countryside? Scared children wrested from their parents while the Germans made craters of *their* homes? She was in no state. And anyway, why should she protect strangers' children?

"No one protected our houseful," she said.

"What's that?" Mr. Watson said.

"I said," she started loudly. But her voice faltered. "I said, Thank you, Mr. Watson."

She hadn't the Blitz spirit at all. People like this Mrs. Arbuthnot did their bit, taking on more than required. Collecting scrap and mending old clothes into new, firewatching at night. But instead of feeling expansive and generous as some seemed to, Bridget could only turn her back and curl over the softest parts of herself.

The matron had her dead to rights. *Closed fist.* Which is what worried her.

"All right, love?" Mr. Watson said.

If she stayed without her pay packet, she'd have to find a cheaper place to live while she looked for more work, and not the kind of work her mam had wanted for her. Not the kind she wanted for herself. If she stayed, she had no way to get back into the nursing scheme. No hospital in London would take her without some sort of acknowledgment of where she'd spent the war so far—and, beyond that, word would be out soon. Matron might keep the news out of the 'papers but not from the vine that twisted among nurses' dormitories. She would never be able to walk into another infirmary without wondering who knew, who had heard.

Not that she expected this Mrs. Arbuthnot to take her on— how could she? On the matron's reference, who thought her a killer? The envelope smudged with blood couldn't be an endorsement.

She needed a fresh start. In the country, if necessary, untethered. She gathered the letter and the telephone exchange. The number would reach Mrs. Arbuthnot, with or without the letter. How urgently did the woman need help?

Bridget turned her attention to the cold hearth. "Mr. Watson, shall I bring you a cup of tea?"

He didn't answer for a moment. He would die in that room

someday. Is that what she waited for here in London? More death? Her own?

"Aye," Mr. Watson said. "Tea would be grand."

"With milk? I've got just enough, I think."

"You're too kind to me, Bridget."

While the fire under the kettle caught on the kindling of the matron's letter, Bridget went to the cupboard and brought down two cups. She had exactly two, mismatched from the charity shop, one chipped at the rim. She liked it even so. It was her own, something that had not come from the ashes of her old life.

When she served Mr. Watson in his room, and sat at his rickety little table for company, she thought about taking care of children again. She couldn't love them, obviously. It went without saying. But she saved Mr. Watson the last of the milk and took the chipped cup for herself.

-3-

BRIDGET KELLY

Mrs. Mitchell's rooming house, near
Regent's Park, London

Bridget had been in bed an hour when thudding along the landing woke her. She sat up, confused, hearing shouts and voices, the sirens wailing. She threw on her cape, slid her feet into her shoes, and opened the door to find Mr. Patel, who lived in the back apartment and worked for Mrs. Mitchell—some said lived with Mrs. Mitchell—helping Mr. Watson gather himself. Bridget took the gentleman's other arm across her shoulder.

In chaos, she could be calm. Mrs. Mitchell thought it the result of her nurse's training, but Bridget knew the roiling sea was within. Nothing outside could hurt her, and if it tried, it hardly mattered.

The boarders hurried as best they could to the back garden where the corrugated arch of Mrs. Mitchell's Anderson shelter had been sunk into the ground. Under it, there was room enough for everyone, just, but they were forced into close quarters, shoulder to shoulder, knee to knee. Barely acquainted in proper fashion over Mrs. Mitchell's everyday china, they were strangers dressed in shadows and bedclothes, trying not to look one another in the eye.

They helped Mr. Watson to the bench and then Mr. Patel crouched at the door with the lantern. They had enough fuel for an hour or two. "It'll be another false alarm," he said. He glanced toward Mrs. Mitchell.

Bridget sat at the other side of Mr. Watson.

"Or it *won't* be a false alarm," said one of the widowed sisters who commanded the large double room at the front of the house, all the best views. They were Mrs. Henshaw and Mrs. Barden, but Bridget hadn't sorted them out in her mind. "Few of those to be had."

The groan of aeroplanes approached.

"And we'll be forced into another night in this trench," the other sister said.

"Better this trench than one in Belgium, Mrs. Henshaw," Mr. Watson said. "Or a grave."

Bridget couldn't look around to see which was Mrs. Henshaw. The Anderson was too tight quarters, not enough air. It was theater, tucking in like this. The Anderson in the garden of the old place was a twist of metal now, as much good as it had done. She closed her eyes and tried to keep still.

Mr. Watson said, "And for the unlucky, the trenches they dig will serve both purposes."

"Weren't you in the war, Mr. Watson?" Mrs. Mitchell said.

The sisters sighed and Bridget nearly gagged. To keep from turning herself inside out like the dead soldier at St. Prisca's took all her concentration. The effort she put in, she might as well be willing the 'planes above to stay in the sky.

"In the war to end all wars—quite wrong about that, we were—I was a young man and saw a bit of the continent," Mr. Watson said. There was a rustling as he sat up straighter. "They sent us in railway cars to France with some of their funny words on the side, so we started calling ourselves after them. Omms and Chevoos."

"Men and . . . horses?" said one of the sisters.

"Right you are," Mr. Watson said. "Forty men or eight horses, that's the top-off on one of those railcars. We didn't know the words, then, of course. Didn't know anything. Just went where they said and shot who they said to shoot." He stared into the dark corner of the shelter for a moment. "Bah," he said. "What are memories for? I have my souvenir. I earned my metal—"

"Oh?" Mrs. Mitchell sat forward. "A medal?"

"Metal, my dear lady. Iron rations in me leg."

"Oh," she said.

"It's no longer painful, I hope?" Mr. Patel said.

"Only when it rains, Mr. Patel," Mr. Watson said. It rained all the time.

One of the sisters jumped in, "If that was the worst you got—"

Antiaircraft guns thudded not far away. The 'planes raged overhead, the strikes banging like the world's largest tin drum, shaking the ground. Dust came down from the seams of the Anderson.

"No, indeed," Mr. Watson said after a few minutes. "No, not the worst by far."

Bridget cringed into the shadows. Must she brace herself even further to hear of fallen comrades? Every soldier in hospital had wanted to tell her their stories, but they never wondered about hers.

But Mr. Watson had said all he would tonight.

Mr. Patel held up the lantern. "We should save the fuel. It might be a long night."

No one said anything. Mr. Patel snuffed the light and they sat in the dark, the permission to speak gone out, too. Waiting for the all-clear, Bridget could imagine she sat in another shelter, that the breathing in the dark belonged to those she longed for.

The signal finally came to return to their beds and Bridget and the others trudged in. The air tasted of dust, from the plasterboard of crushed homes. Dust and smoke.

Bridget spent the rest of the night turning from one side to the other, mashing her pillow into new shapes, thinking of the dead soldier from St. Prisca's.

He'd been a young one, probably ambitious and eager. He'd have signed on knowing the dangers, but never predicting the death that had come for him.

In all her plans for nursing, she had never considered she might harm someone.

Bridget spent the early hours as light crept in around the blackout shades going through her actions of the prior day, over and again until she thought she might go mad. Was already mad.

At barely a decent hour, the doorbell sounded. Mr. Watson's voice came through the wall.

"Our man Tom again," he said. He would be at the window, an early riser. "Very ardent."

Bridget dressed quickly and went to the parlor to receive him. When they met, he took her hand and kissed her temple. To avoid her lipstick, she had once thought. "Did you have some trouble last night?" he said. "Aunt says she was in the garden shelter again?"

Tom's aunt had been their landlady at the old home place down the street. She still lived near, a rented room. Acting the displaced royal with the owner, was Bridget's guess.

"Shall we go for a walk?"

"It's rather cold out, Bridget, and anyway, I'm in a dreadful rush," Tom said. He seemed to be performing for an audience, as though he knew the entire house listened in. Tom had a soft face, a soft middle, but a loud voice, like someone trained for the stage. An only child. "Just a few minutes to spare," he said. "Only I came to tell you I'm off this morning. I've new orders."

"So have I," she said.

He dropped her hand and recovered to a normal level of voice. "How do you mean?"

"Well, not this morning, but soon. Top secret."

"You're such a kid sometimes," he said. "Look, I'll write to you."

"I won't be here," she said. "I told you. I'm going on a mission of charity."

Tom stared dully at her. "What about nursing?"

"There are plenty of nurses," Bridget said, making it up as she went along and startled to hear the words coming out of her mouth. She had decided to go. "But I've a special assignment. Specially chosen." She did feel like a child and wished she'd never said anything of it. "Tommy," she said. "Do you plan to marry me?"

"I thought—well, that's rather—" He pulled at his neck, looking to the doorway in case Mrs. Mitchell stood by. "I didn't realize—"

"Several of the girls on the ward have been hitched up quickly before their men went to France." But she didn't want to talk about St. Prisca's. "Just something I thought of."

"I thought—"

"Wouldn't you rather I was taken care of? Just in case?"

Something passed over his face. "Wouldn't you rather be a wife than a widow?"

"Of course, but. At the moment I'm neither." That was the problem. She was nothing.

"It's only an office in Bedfordshire I'm off to," he said, his voice now quiet. "I'll be back in a week—"

"Never mind. I only thought I could be sure of something."

"None of us can be sure of anything anymore." He glanced at her from the corner of his eye. "Are you really on some sort of assignment?"

"You're doubting me. It's not enough to break my heart?"

"If I thought you were serious . . ."

He might do it, he might propose, and then where would she be? "I'm teasing," she said.

He looked relieved. "You shouldn't, not when I feel as I do, and when you—I shouldn't say."

"You can say what you like." If he said something that cut the binds and spilled her out, then perhaps it was for the best.

But he wouldn't. "I'd rather not. Let's part as friends, at least."

"Be safe, Tommy," she said. Bedfordshire.

"You'll write me? And send me a photo?"

He would do better to find a snap left behind in some bombed-out house. A photograph of her would impress no one.

"I'll send an address when I know it." Bridget turned her cheek for the kiss that would not touch her lips. She wished she loved him. It would have been far easier if only she could.

-4-

BRIDGET KELLY

Paddington Station, two days later

They were late leaving London.

Not on the day, of course. London still ran nearly on time, as well as it could. The Underground dislodged those sleeping on the Tube platforms every morning, switched on the electric, and started up again, no problem there. The trains into and out of the city still ran, a point of pride. That was the British way, everything suffered with a certain dignity—or a lie the papers would have them believe.

Bridget had decided on dignity for herself, as well. She was punctual, pressed, her best court shoes shined. The nurse's navy wool cape brushed and hair tightly pinned under a hat from two seasons ago couldn't be helped. The white cap she'd taken was tucked in with her things, something to wish on. She needed Mrs. Arbuthnot's good favor to return to London exultant, and she would have it.

In the crush of travelers, soldiers, and porters, she found the correct platform and set down the dressing case borrowed from Mr. Watson. It was nearly empty. Steam from the train had made the station hot, the air thick.

Nearby a woman crouched on her heels in front of a young

boy, her face hidden by the wide curved brim of a red picture hat. Her Sunday best. Bridget turned away as the woman pressed the boy to her dark cloak like a lover, shoulders shaking.

No, it was a bright early morning, the train already waiting. But they were late in the *season* of escape, weren't they? The evacuations had begun the week war was declared, some children having to be sent out a second time once the bombing finally began. Thousands of children—hundreds of thousands, by now—had already been sent away from London for their safety.

Bridget looked for the time, tried not to make an accounting as she waited. If her biggest little sisters had gone with their school. If her mam had taken the babies to shelter somewhere else. If—

It never ended.

It *would* never end, if she let light in through the crack. She folded her arms around herself.

Along the platform marched a woman stuffed into a severe gray suit with gold buttons, trailed by two porters and a white-haired man wearing a beret, of all things. The woman's hat was small, pointed, and set too far forward, the sort of thing the probationers at St. Prisca's discussed as a character flaw. This woman hadn't the delicacy for fashion. She walked chest first, moving like the prow of a destroyer slicing through waves. The woman directed her hat toward Bridget and looked her over with less satisfaction than Bridget thought she deserved. "Which one are you?" she said. This was Mrs. Arbuthnot.

"Bridget Kelly, missus."

She was older than Bridget's mam would have been, but not a lady of leisure from the Woman's Voluntary, or if she was indeed, a different sort than Bridget had imagined. The woman's appraisal had moved on toward the mother and son on the platform. "Pleasantries later, if there's time after the other one arrives," she said. "Now I've raised five of my own, and when the time comes to part them, I'm afraid it will be difficult. Be gentle but firm. This is their child's last chance for safety, and they must understand the sacrifice, though difficult to bear, is necessary."

The man in the beret caught up. "They'll have the best of care, all the comforts. Far more satisfactory than they have at home, I wager."

"Malcolm, please," Mrs. Arbuthnot said. She turned back to Bridget. "My husband. You *will* be able to manage the mothers?"

The two porters arrived, weighed down. "I'll have that," Mr. Arbuthnot said, reaching to extract a small parcel from one of the helpers and nearly bungling the job for all. "What time do we arrive, darling? Joan? Where's the easel?"

"Sent ahead with the cots, Malcolm," Mrs. Arbuthnot said. "Don't fuss." She went to see to the mother and son.

He would, though, Bridget could see that. In no time he would gain permission to board early and have everything just as he liked.

Mr. Arbuthnot caught her staring. "Lucky getaway, eh?" he said. "Nearly criminal."

"Pardon me?" Had Matron Bailey had a change of heart? Had she telephoned Mrs. Arbuthnot herself?

"*Paid* to get out of the city as it falls down around your ears."

"Oh. Yes, sir." If the children would only arrive.

Mrs. Arbuthnot's voice rose over the noise of the station. "Mrs. Poole, I beg you!"

The mother in the red hat brushed past with the boy in tow and now Bridget caught a glimpse of her face, puffy and blotched from emotion.

"I'd rather he died alongside me," the woman cried over her shoulder, "than be left behind with no one." The linen identification tag on the child's coat fluttered behind.

"Mrs. Poole," Mrs. Arbuthnot called. "Please be sensible!"

The woman's hat disappeared quickly into the crowds.

"Silly woman," Mrs. Arbuthnot said under her breath. "Selfish woman. You see what we're up against, everyone losing their heads." She tugged the hem of her jacket. "Where *is* the other girl?"

"I don't know," Bridget whispered, the mother's words still clanging around in her head. *I'd rather he died alongside me.* How often she had wished—

"Oh, the children," Mrs. Arbuthnot exclaimed. "Here they are."

The children were tots, baby fat in their knees below shorts and skirts, socks pulled up or sliding, shoes scuffed or untied. They had tags affixed to their coats and child-sized gas masks in paper cases on straps around their necks. They wore caps and hats or bonnets and flung them to the ground in a tantrum. Those who were carried by their mums kicked to be let down. Two were *infants*, dear God.

Porters followed behind with pillowslips stuffed, picnic hampers, tiny cases ridiculous in large hands. Very few fathers were in evidence. Fathers were at the front, or already in hospital, or worse. It was best not to think of fathers.

Some carried bears or dolls or toy 'planes or tanks. Each child was allowed a favorite. As the platform filled, a young boy stopped running his pet locomotive along his mother's sleeve and looked on the soft toys the girls carried with hungry eyes. Comfort, too, would be rationed.

Mrs. Arbuthnot managed the group, her jacket riding up, her hat sliding further over her eye. The mothers had questions about visits, where they might send packages, telephone calls, visits again. Mrs. Arbuthnot reassured them and pulled Bridget aside as though for further instructions but actually to take a break from the mothers. "I can't imagine what's keeping the other nurse," she huffed.

"The other *nurse*." Bridget glanced down at herself, at the cloak she should have left behind. She hadn't meant to pass herself off as anything other than short-term help. Had the advertisement asked specifically for a nurse? Or was she to be rather a nanny? "Did the other—girl come recommended by Matron Bailey, as well?"

"Now don't be jealous. Your matron's good opinion of you is enough for me," Mrs. Arbuthnot said. "The other girl came through another source altogether."

Mr. Arbuthnot gestured to catch his wife's attention, his long coat flapping. "Yes, Malcolm, I see the time," she said.

"Mine is lost," Bridget said.

"What is?"

"My reference. My letter from Matron Bailey."

"Oh yes. I should have to request another one, I suppose."

Bridget tried to think of a way to discourage it. She had only wanted the new beginning, to leave all the blood of St. Prisca's behind her.

"It's too late now," Mrs. Arbuthnot said. "As you can see, we're under siege."

Bridget turned to find the platform rather crowded. "How many—"

"What I hoped for were extra hands at the oars, but I'm afraid we'll have to make do until new arrangements might be made," Mrs. Arbuthnot said. "It's time to board them, Nurse Kelly. Look sharp but be gentle—with the *mothers*, mind."

Nurse Kelly.

This development just as Bridget was meant to take control of the situation, to give the families confidence in her abilities to keep and care, to administer and tuck in, to guard, of course, to keep safe from the enemy, to serve tea and milk, to know proper temperatures and procedures. She should grab the porter who had taken her case and let the group go on without her. Could they? She imagined all the women yanking their children home, all those children *to die alongside* in London—and the matron hearing from Mrs. Arbuthnot, an earful.

"Nurse Kelly?" Mrs. Arbuthnot said.

She should be grasping hands and leading the 'vacs into the carriage, but Bridget had suddenly remembered doing much the same, one sister's hand on her left, another's on her right, off to church, off to market. *Home.*

Die alongside them.

She might never come back, that was it. She might never see the family grave again. That's what this woman was asking of her, to go without knowing what lay ahead, another item on the list to go without. Stockings, beef, her family, her livelihood, and now assurances.

The mothers said good-bye and then good-bye again, tousling curls and cradling until Mrs. Arbuthnot insinuated herself between a mum and child and motioned for Bridget to take the infant.

Bridget kept her face right and led the parade up the steps into the chocolate-and-cream-colored carriage. Inside, she sorted the children onto two benches, one on each side of the train, detaching mothers from children and sending them back out. All the while trying not to let her mind wander toward Regent's Square and everything familiar. Out of nowhere she thought briefly of Tom, of letters that may never reach her. Wherever she was going—the departure boards listed no town names, of course, the way of the world—there was no guarantee, not of His Majesty's postal service, nor of survival.

-5-

BRIDGET

A few minutes to departure

Bridget bounced an infant on her hip, wishing for a last gulp of London air—or an escape back to the city streets before the train lurched forward and made the decision for her. *You are not a nurse.*

Through the window, Bridget spotted the red, curved hat brim of the young mother who'd taken her son away. The woman had hooked a conductor and now gestured wildly at the train as he shook his head.

Madam changed her mind, did she?

But wouldn't Mrs. Arbuthnot be pleased to have the boy along?

Bridget hurried to the doorway and signaled until the harassed conductor looked up.

"There's still time, isn't there, sir?" Bridget said. "Madam, where is your son?"

The woman turned, the curve of her hat lifting to reveal a haughty face instead of a grieving one. "Pardon?" This woman was a few years older than Bridget, her red hat rather more posh than Mrs. Poole's had been. She had a cool manner, not the moist cheeks of a mother saying her good-byes, and cut a sleek figure with her dark cape thrown back over her shoulders, the bright red lining framing her slim skirt. Bridget felt dowdy, everything about her dull. Even in the same cape—

"Oh, you're the other *nurse*." Bridget stepped off the train, and the mother of the infant she carried came near again to kiss and cry and pet. "We've only been waiting for you all this time."

The woman in the red hat looked at the baby, the mother. "I *am* sorry. I got caught up, as I was just explaining to this gentleman—"

"You can make your apologies to Mrs. Arbuthnot, but you should hurry."

"They say the train is full."

"It's been arranged. Mrs. Arbuthnot has it all sorted. Come now, I need your help straightaway." She couldn't very well see to two infants and a brood of under-fives all the way to the countryside. The Arbuthnots had first-class tickets, and she knew Mr. Arbuthnot would not be putting in a hand once they arrived.

The other nurse's bag was seen to and then she followed Bridget into the carriage. "And what's your name?" the other nurse said.

"I'm Bridget Kelly."

"That's me, as well," the other said delightedly, leaning down to look out the window as they went. "Isn't that something?"

"I had five Bridgets in my year at school," Bridget said. "And rather quite a lot of Kellys."

They dodged passengers and cases up the aisle to where Mrs. Arbuthnot tried to make herself heard to the ticket inspector over the shrieks of the other infant trying to launch himself from her arms.

"Here she is, missus," Bridget said. "You didn't mention we were both Bridget Kelly."

Mrs. Arbuthnot, frowning, handed the baby into Bridget's empty arm.

"Young lady—" When she looked upon the other Bridget, Mrs. Arbuthnot's words ran out. The other nurse was no girl, clearly, and, in addition to being the kind of glamorous that made the ticket inspector blush, she had the sharpish look of a woman who wouldn't be scolded.

"At sixes and sevens, Mrs. Arbuthnot," the other Bridget said. "My sincerest apologies."

"Ah, yes," Mrs. Arbuthnot said, finding herself again. "Did you say you were Bridget Kelly as well?"

"We can do a rota, which one of us gets to be Bridget Kelly." Bridget had a crying baby on each hip, and a stitch in her back. She glanced toward the rest of the children, who played with each other's toys, examined the next train over through the window, waved to mums on the platform. She counted heads, losing track as they moved about.

"Well, you both can't be Bridget," Mrs. Arbuthnot said. "It will be confusing for the children. And the staff."

"The staff?" The other Bridget's cool regard split open into a smile. She had a deep dimple in her cheek that drew the eye. It was a powerful force, armed to destroy like one of Hitler's secret weapons. She reached up and pulled off the red hat, revealing smooth, dark hair and high cheekbones. Bridget didn't need to be told how she would come out in the comparison of one Bridget Kelly to the other.

"I'm Bridey at home, missus." It was out before she could think.

"Then it shall be," Mrs. Arbuthnot said. "Thank you, Bridey."

It stung a bit, the old baby name drawn out from the attics. The *children* would call her that name. She didn't feel herself, suddenly. Wasn't herself.

"Everyone calls me Gigi," said the other nurse. The dimple still sunk into her cheek.

Bridget stared. Another battlefront of the war had opened up before her very eyes. They hadn't even left the station and here this one had already given herself an adventuring name.

"Gigi, is it?" The slash of Mrs. Arbuthnot's lips pursed into something short of a smile. "Those names will do for the children, at least. Please go see to them, and I'll have further instructions when we get near our destination."

"Where is that final address again?" Gigi said. "Mrs. Arbuthnot? Ma'am?" Mrs. Arbuthnot would not be commanded back.

Bridget—now Bridey and a good deal sorry she had offered to be called it—pushed one of the infants at Gigi.

"I didn't—" The other woman took the child awkwardly and followed Bridey toward their benches.

"I didn't reckon for babies, either," Bridey said over her shoulder. The matron had said under-fives, and she had pictured them all four years old, like a set, standard and tidy. "And no one ever said *ten*."

"Ten? *Ten* children?"

They arrived at their benches, the children clambering and inquisitive. When would the train leave, when would they have tea, when would they arrive, where were they going. Passengers along the carriage turned to look.

"Ten," Bridey said. Ten little lives in their hands, and herself a loaded weapon. The infant in her arms screeched. Bridget sat heavily as the train gasped into motion and raised the child over her shoulder.

"Good *night*." Gigi sat on the bench opposite. "Did she tell *you* where we're headed?"

"The countryside, that's all I know."

"The West Country, isn't it? Cream and chocolate cars."

"Oh." She hadn't thought to ask and what did it say about her? That she trusted her betters, or that she had no option but to go along?

Outside the window, mothers lined the platform, the entire length. The children crushed into place at the glass to wave to their mums, who ran alongside, and then to other mums they didn't know.

Bridget held herself still. The children would need her to be stoic.

When they were past the end of the platform, the children strained to see backward. At last they sat back on the benches, stunned as cows, questions at an end. They plucked at the violet fabric of the bench seat, some crying, some trying not to.

"Hush now, hush," Bridget whispered, jostling the one against her neck until it stopped caterwauling. She had helped with her brother and sisters, and she knew what she was about, nurse or no. If she needed to be skilled with children, then she would be. She could be anything she needed to be.

The train was picking up steam, and so were some of the children, in misery. "Let's be brave soldiers," she said. "For Mummy and Dad."

"And for King and country," Gigi said, not soothingly, more like she was raising a pint in a pub. She held the infant out from her as he began to pucker and scream, pink as a ham. "And in payment for all our sins thus far. Are you quite mad? You volunteered for this?"

"So did you," Bridey said. A warbling sort of laugh escaped her, and all the children looked her way, wiping noses on sleeves, smiling to themselves at the sound. They were innocents caught up with whatever she had agreed to, whomever she had decided to be. *Absolutely vigilant.* Yes, she would have to be.

-6-

BRIDEY

Somewhere southwest of London

The train passed out of London and its outskirts, laundry hung in back gardens, and then finally into fields with hedges, through smaller towns, each station with its name painted over. Then after an extended delay at a large town with church spires and hills, the train took a sharp turn, shadows dragging across the carriage to a new angle. The afternoon grew long, the view remote and empty.

Gigi begged off for the toilet and didn't come back. Meanwhile the children teased, kicked, cried, or turned inward. They had a messy tea right at their seats from the baskets. Bridey handed out biscuits for a makeshift pudding after, wiped dribbles from jackets, and dusted crumbs from the smocked fronts of dresses. When Mrs. Arbuthnot came by to check on them, they had turns at the toilet.

"Where's the other one?" Mrs. Arbuthnot said. "This Gigi."

"I'm sure she'll be back soon, missus." It was a train. Surely the nurse hadn't hopped off at the last stop, leaving them in the lurch. Bridey might better be able to pretend she was a real nurse if she weren't bothered by the constant companionship of the genuine article, but she hoped against it, anyway. She would need the help.

Mrs. Arbuthnot went back to her carriage, and Bridget changed nappies on the bench, ignoring glares from nearby passengers. It was a frantic business keeping all ten in order, and she was wilting, one infant wailing against her neck, the other propped against her on the bench, matching volume.

A man with striking blue eyes passed by, giving her a wink for her troubles. *The cheek.*

She got the babies settled and started a story for the older set, winding the tale out until all of them slept. The infants were tucked into a nest made of her cloak, and the rest of them draped across the bench or leaned against the window or cuddled together. It could be done, just, if this Gigi could be expected to take her allotment.

Now here was the Bridget Kelly the matron had spoken of. Keen-eyed and keeping score. She couldn't begin thinking of the children as bandages needing to be wrapped, dressings needing to be changed. Bridey looked down at the girl against her hip. The identification tag tied to the girl's coat button read *Doreen*, written in delicate, shaking script. She was a living doll, with a rosebud mouth and silken hair like something from a fairy tale.

Doreen should have reminded Bridget of her littlest sister, but that young one had been rather a skinny, sallow child, not unlike the foundlings at the hospital near their old flat. *These* children were loved and looked after, still fat at the thighs and wrists from mother's milk.

These children had loving parents. Among them, *Bridget* was the foundling.

She reached down and pulled Doreen into her lap as she would her sewing or embroidery. Something to keep herself weighted down, to keep the flutter beginning in her stomach from turning into tremors. Doreen's eyelids lifted, fought to stay open, and lost.

Gigi came along the aisle. She'd been gone an hour.

"Where have you been?" Bridget said, sounding more cross than she'd meant to.

"Chatting with some blokes I met in the next carriage."

"I'll need your *help*—"

"Of course." She looked over the scene of sleeping children. "You seem to have it in hand. What do you need me to do?"

Bridey watched the countryside roll by, fuming. The girl Doreen was warm against her, and her eyes pricked with the effects of the last two days, readying for the journey and fighting off visions of the soldier from St. Prisca's each night. The lost sleep of several months of grief, more than a year of war. She closed her eyes.

Then Bridey jolted awake, finding the carriage dark. She sat up with a gasp.

"Tunnel," Gigi said.

They were out of it in two seconds, Bridey's eyes now dazzled by the light. She'd only dozed off. "I didn't mean to fall asleep."

"You didn't miss anything," Gigi said. "Except—" She lowered her voice and leaned across the aisle. "Some high drama two rows along."

Bridey looked among the benches until she spotted a couple sitting together but leaning apart, allowing more space between them than was proper, given how full the train was. They weren't much older than Bridey, perhaps still courting or—

"Do you think they've left that seat for the Holy Spirit?" Gigi said. "They disagree on nearly everything."

"Married, then," Bridey said. "How have you managed to learn what they agree or disagree about? Impressive range for eavesdropping, and their backs to you."

Gigi shrugged. "I chatted them up a bit earlier. But you picked them out, as well, and based on what?"

Bridey looked them over again. "Posture, I suppose. And—"

"Yes?"

"They're not reading anything or chatting or dozing or looking out the window. They're only *not* speaking to one another."

"That's rather good. You'd make a good one for—well, have you heard of Mass-Observation? I did some work for them."

Bridey hadn't. "Mass-*Observation*? It sounds rather . . ."

"Doesn't it?" Gigi whispered. "It's anthropology, only not in New Guinea or some other far-off place—here."

Now it did sound rather troublesome. "They're studying the culture of . . . us? In aid of what?"

"For the sake of—of the Register, for the record of what it is to be British. For instance, when Edward abdicated. We collected then. The coronation, after? We collected."

"Collected?" Bridey said, her voice rather high and too loud. "Collected what precisely?"

Gigi's eyes shifted up the carriage and back. "Opinions. Attitudes. They had a lot to say about the war posters, what people will respond to, that sort of thing. If you know what the nation's citizens think, you can better talk with them."

"If you know what people think, you can better change their minds to what you'd have them think."

Gigi sat back. "Could do. And here I thought all that work was used down the line to, I don't know, sell soap flakes. Don't concern yourself. I don't do such work anymore."

Except she clearly did, for her own amusement. Gigi's keen powers of observation wouldn't work in Bridey's favor. How soon? How soon before she revealed herself as a fraud?

Mrs. Arbuthnot came along the aisle, tsking at the girl

curled into Bridey's lap. "Don't pet them, girls. It doesn't do for them to get attached or to expect to be mollycoddled."

Bridey smartened herself as best she could, sliding Doreen off her skirt. "You said you have five children, missus?"

"*Five*," Gigi said, looking Mrs. Arbuthnot over as though she were a prize heifer.

The woman's face, already stone, had nowhere to go. "They weren't raised pampered little royals, I can tell you."

Bridey recognized it then. Under the airs and graces, Mrs. Arbuthnot had a hint of the wide accent of the working classes, same as Bridey's mam.

"All I'm saying is that you'll not have lap enough for them all," Mrs. Arbuthnot said, prim once more. "Better to teach them to . . ." She searched the fields rushing by for the right term.

"Buck up?" Gigi said.

"Something of that nature," Mrs. Arbuthnot said, turning to include her. Gigi was freshening the pins in her hair. She had lovely long fingernails. Bridey fixed upon them for a moment, wondering how she had managed to keep them. Matron Bailey had strict ideas about such things, and they broke often enough besides.

"It's our duty," Mrs. Arbuthnot was saying, "to make sure these children don't go back to their parents ruined by our influence."

Gigi's dimple threatened. "Which influence is that, ma'am?"

"They should be molded into proper British citizens," Mrs. Arbuthnot said. "It's a big job. We're doing nothing less than saving England, girls. Don't let anyone tell you otherwise."

Without Doreen on her lap, Bridey felt light and didn't recognize herself in Mrs. Arbuthnot's speech. Didn't recognize *children*, either. One would think, if she had raised *five* . . .

Gigi, across the aisle, tried to hide the dimple that gave away she was smiling.

"Bridey, you look as though there's something you want to say," Mrs. Arbuthnot said.

"Well, missus, I—children pulled from the rubble of their own nurseries," Bridey said, swallowing hard to get through it. "They've been known to have the same shock as soldiers pulled from the battlefield. Don't you think small ones might . . . buck up a little more stoutly if they feel safe?"

Mrs. Arbuthnot swayed with the train for a moment. "Is that your training speaking, Bridget? Or life experience at age, what, twenty?"

So she would be Bridget, then, when she needed to be reminded of her place. She was nineteen. And to speak of her training—she should keep her mouth shut, good and proper, and let Mrs. Arbuthnot tell her how she wanted things done. "Four sisters and a brother, missus," she said. "I—"

"And do cuddles make your siblings safe when bombs scream overhead, Bridget?"

She couldn't think of it and deflected the woman's words by sinking deeply inside her own skin. "No, missus."

"Don't love them, girls," Mrs. Arbuthnot said, turning toward the first-class carriage. "A few less hearts broken, in the end."

Gigi leaned into the aisle to watch their employer march away, then turned back to Bridey. "In the *end*?" she said, stretching her mouth to mimic Mrs. Arbuthnot's revealed accent. "When the devil will that be, I wonder?"

The other nurse was sharp, much too sharp. Bridey turned to the window, wondering if her only allies would be the children, or if she should have any at all.

BRIDEY

On the train

After a long afternoon of hedges and stone walls, of vast stretches of farmland dotted by sheep, of pausing at stations to let more important trains pass, trains full with soldiers or the wounded, of delays and more tunnels, they ran alongside a vast stretch of water. Gigi leaned over the aisle to study the view on Bridey's side.

"That's the sea," she said. "Does it make sense to take your charges to the *sea*side?"

Her charges, as though Gigi had never signed on for the work.

The train turned inland along a river, the tide out to reveal mudflats. Seabirds whirled overhead.

The children played or fretted, asked questions she tried to answer or questions she didn't answer, fought over toys, shared a snack, stared out the window in awe or dismay. "What is that?" one of the little boys asked of the landscape, once again dry. Flat, vast, and empty.

"Absolutely nothing at all," Gigi said.

"I wonder if it's the moors," Bridey said.

"How very Wuthering Heights."

"Eh?"

Gigi shook her head, her attention turned on two men and a woman coming down the aisle toward them.

"We thought you'd jumped the caboose," one of the men said, strolling with hands in his trouser pockets. Gigi, he meant. He was fresh-faced and jovial, while the other man was brooding and angled, the muscles in his jaw reminding Bridey of the skinless drawings in the *Gray's Anatomy* she'd seen at St. Prisca's. The woman had glossy red lips and a curvaceous figure. Something about her made Bridey think they'd met before. Was she from St. Prisca's? Or the old lane? Bridey turned her head to the window.

"I told you I'd have to get back to *work*," Gigi said. "I have responsibilities. With the children."

The group made themselves at home in between the sleeping children. The woman perched on the seat arm, her skirt riding up on shapely legs. She had a farmgirl's face, suntanned and freckled, but short black hair, modern and set into waves. She looked over the scene of their benches. "Quite a few responsibilities," she said. "*Too* many."

The jolly man wore a silver tie pin tipped with a sparkling bauble that might be worth something, but his shirt collar was too wide for his neck, his jacket too loose in the shoulders. One could tell a great deal about a man by his clothes. The ill-tempered one, for instance, dressed like a boy home from university, a bush jacket that did nothing to give him any shape.

The friendly one leaned across the aisle to include Bridey when he caught her looking. "How do you do?"

It was the blue-eyed man who'd stopped to have a wink at her expense. "Just fine, thank you." She turned her chin toward the window again, the only proper thing.

"Bridey, this chap reckons we're going to South Devon," Gigi said. "We've passed Newton Abbot already."

"My ticket's for Paignton," the jovial man said. "But the line goes as far as a place called Kingswear."

"As remote an outpost as you can imagine, then?" said the brooding one.

"You might continue to Dartmouth on a ferry from there. For a bit of *society*," the first said. He stretched out his legs, taking up as much space as he could and kicking his dour friend in the knee with the toe of his battered brogue.

"Surely we'll alight before that," Gigi said. "What do you think, Bridey?"

They all took up too much space. Bridey looked up and down the aisle for a ticket inspector to move them along. "Surely we'll find out when we get there," she said. "If you could be careful of the children, please."

"Here now," another man's voice said.

Bridey thought he would be the inspector, but the voice belonged to another passenger, a man in a blue pinstripe suit who hurried along the aisle, not caring how the other passengers turned to stare. "Look out for the little ones, will you?" he said.

The winking man gave his apologies; the woman stood to go. The gloomy one grinned into his own chest.

"I hope they weren't bothering you," the new arrival said. He wasn't handsome but was well made. His suit was pre-war, pre-restrictions, with cuffs on the trousers and a matching waistcoat—a smart look that signaled he cared more for the war effort than new fashion or money spent. He carried a walking stick that had the look of a simple branch stripped of its bark, and seemed to need it for a hitch in his left leg.

"They weren't," Gigi said.

"*Thank* you, sir," Bridey said. "It's already such a lot of work to keep ten children organized."

"You're doing a splendid job," he said, turning to gaze over the sleeping children. He had fresh shrapnel scarring on his neck, red and angry. A vet, home. "War nursery, is it?"

"Yes, sir."

"Thank heavens for women like you . . ." He leaned forward and reached out his hand.

"Bridget Kelly, sir," she said, standing to save him the stretch.

"Thank you, Miss Kelly. Nurse Kelly, I mean to say," he said, noticing her cloak. "Llewelyn Nevins."

There was the problem of rank. He'd be a lieutenant at least. "Thank *you*, sir."

"Ah, yes. Home a bit earlier than planned." He tapped his walking stick once on the floor. "Our boys will get the job done in the end and these children will be alive to see it. Thank you for seeing to these little angels while their mums and daddies see us all through it."

He couldn't know that what he said to her was both exactly what she would want and almost too much to bear. "Thank you," she said. "Our employer says we're saving England."

The young woman rolled her red lips to keep from laughing. She turned toward the back of the train and the others followed, the ill-mannered one, the ill-humored one, all moving along the train sampling the headlines of strangers' newspapers, commenting on a book someone held, asking someone the time, drawing attention and reveling in it. The whole of the train for their amusement.

"We'll do it any way we can, won't we?" the man said. "Have a pleasant journey, Nurse Kelly, and good luck to you." He walked off toward the first-class car.

"What drivel," Gigi said as soon as he was gone. She stood.

"Where are you going now?" Bridey said.

"Powder my nose," Gigi said.

"Take one of the girls with—" But Gigi didn't wait to be told how she might take a shift.

Bridget was left to sputter and merely think the things she couldn't say.